"I've loved watching Chuck perform onstage. These limericks reveal a different creativity. They're so engaging and warm-hearted and downright funny. They're close to being addictive—like those potato chips, there's no way to read just one!"

—**Chris Fabry** Christy Award winner, author of more than 80 books and host of Chris Fabry Live on Moody Radio.

"I love funny, talented people, and Chuck Neighbors is one of my favorites. Whether he's performing a one-man dramatic play, a comedy monologue, or appearing in an original sketch that he's written, Chuck has entertained audiences all across this nation and beyond. Now, he's turned his attention to writing books. ***Get Me To The Church In Rhyme*** *is Chuck's collection of humorous limericks covering a myriad of topics, all having to do with church life. From the offering to the benediction, from Methodists to Charismatics, Chuck has written about the world of church-goer with great respect and good humor. A fast read for some quick laughs. Now, I just have to wait for Volume #2."*

—**Martha Bolton** Emmy nominated former staff writer for Bob Hope, playwright, and the author of 88 books.

"I travel distances to get to see Chuck Neighbors. His presentations live with me. I remember every performance in detail that I have seen. He is that good. Now, with this book, I take him with me. This begs to be purloined."

—**Gayle Erwin**, Director of Servant Quarters, Author of **The Jesus Style**

Like a homerun
in the ballpark
with good Friends
like Kathy & Mark!
Blessed!

[illegible]

Get Me To The Church in Rhyme

Limericks about God, Faith, and the Church

by Chuck Neighbors

Get Me To The Church In Rhyme

by Chuck Neighbors

For permissions contact:

chuckneighbors@gmail.com

Cover Illustration by Jerry Scairrio

ISBN: 9781687753021

dedication

To the pastors of churches I've known,

Thanks for all the seeds you have sown.

With much admiration

For your inspiration,

May my words bring smile and a groan.

Contents

Contents continued…

foreword

Get Me to the Church in Rhyme.

Limericks—penned in my spare time.

All written by Chuck,

Tryin' to make a buck—

Likely won't make one thin dime.

welcome

Mark tried the new church down the street,

Sat in back, wanting to be discreet,

But they liked to hug.

He came down with a bug

And vowed never again "Meet and Greet."

hymns

The church, well it was divided.

The argument, it was two-sided:

A piano and hymnals,

Or guitars, clanging cymbals?

TWO services it was decided.

solo

The service at church was quite formal,

But the soloist sang with a warble.

The Presbyterian notion

Is to show no emotion.

I tried but I let out a chortle.

baptism

The new pastor was Southern Baptist,

But in dunking was completely hapless.

The convert immersed,

The outcome the worst.

He's now being sued for malpractice.

informal

Phil agreed to give First Church a try,

As he donned his new suit and a tie.

But he felt really dumb,

Kind'a like a sore thumb,

Sitting among the blue jeans and tie-dye.

hell

The church had no affiliation,

No doctrine or views on creation.

On sin, death, and hell,

With a shrug said "oh well."

Their theology's sweeping the nation.

seniors

"Our church is shrinking," they'd whine.

Average age, seventy—a bad sign.

To avert a disaster,

A millennial pastor!

The average is now sixty-nine.

prayer

We believe that prayer is a must.

In faith we praise God and we trust.

Our words are chatter,

It's hearts that matter.

But can we do it without saying "just"?

vegan

Bill needed to learn a new habit

As an Adventist keeping the Sabbath.

The church frowned on meat.

Veggie-links his defeat.

On Monday he was dining on rabbit.

distracted

Reverend John found it grueling to preach.

Little Amy, age five, likes to screech.

Bill snores in his pew.

Cell phones ringing too.

He gave up and fled to the beach.

missions

The missionary was in her prime.

In tongues she would praise all the time!

A surprised Pentecostal,

When the tribe became hostile:

In Swahili—confessed to a crime.

liturgy

An Episcopalian named Cristobal

Had arthritis, his pain was quite visible.

The worst part of liturgy

Was kneeling, such misery!

But with live stream he genuflects digital.

pews

A Methodist named Sue was not nominal.

Her attendance at church was phenomenal.

She once threw a fit

When a stranger did sit

In her pew—oh my! It was comical.

naps

Pastor Todd was Assembly of God.

Exuberant praise was not odd.

If some dared to sleep

He'd shout, spin, and leap.

In worship it's forbidden to nod.

music

Jane was the young instrumentalist

At a church that was fundamentalist.

When she played "Rock of Ages"

The beat was outrageous.

Her dismissal was quick, not the gentlest.

inclusive

The church was progressive, no barrier.

Ben cried, "this is where I will marry her!"

With Belle at the altar

Theology faltered:

Refusing to wed his Welsh Terrier.

politics

All the churches created a treatise:

"Believe this and then you will please us."

Faith's become a big fight

'Tween the left and the right.

Confused—I just want to know Jesus.

technology

Pastor Dawn made an apology,

And blamed it all on technology.

Typing words for the screen

Just emojis were seen,

And no one sang the doxology.

muted

The pastor put on his microphone,

The wireless kind—he should have known.

But unmuted he flushed,

He may even have cussed.

The reaction in church was full-blown.

hippie

There once was a dude name of Skippy;

Who wandered the beach as a hippie.

He thought church a hassle,

Then found Calvary Chapel.

Now he pastors a church in Poughkeepsie.

independence

'Tis the day we celebrate freedom.

Fireworks, and hot dogs—we'll eat 'em.

I'm tempted to brag

As we put up our flag,

Under God? Oh yes, how we need Him!

buildings

There is a new church in Montclair.

The people are hip and have flair.

The building is round

From steeple to ground,

But the sign still says it's "Foursquare."

potluck

The potluck at church was our mission

For fellowship, pies and fried chicken.

Then naive Matthew Reed

Brought in three kinds of weed,

Thus ending this cherished tradition.

social

The church was a great place to meet,

With fellowship there that was sweet.

Now it isn't so nice;

They just use a device

And pass the peace with a tweet.

christmas

Christmas pageant this year—a game changer;

Live critters on stage, there's no danger!

But the donkey would poop,

Prompting Joseph to scoop.

Next year it's away with the manger.

easter

Sunrise service at church before dawn,

It's early and we're stifling a yawn.

Then as we are praying,

The sprinklers start spraying.

Wide awake and baptized on the lawn.

contributions

The ushers all shared disbelief.

Some thought there must be a thief!

But then Elder Kline

Saw donations online.

They all breathed a sigh of relief.

sunday school

In Sunday School poor Mrs. Thrush

Left her classroom in a rush.

You see Larry Long

Read Solomon's Song.

His version made everyone blush.

grace

Pastor Dave, a Lutheran, was humble;

Preached grace—but was known to stumble.

At the Lord's table,

Spilled wine on Aunt Mabel.

"I'm forgiven" he was heard to mumble.

mass

The O'Briens were struggling to cope.

Birth control? They faithfully said "nope."

With eight kids to cherish,

They could start their own parish.

How they wish they'd said "nope" to the Pope.

prosperity

I heard that a preacher named Sam
Promised wealth on his TV program.
Offering prayers for good luck,
Then your pocket he'd pluck.
He fled town and is now on the lam.

trick or treat

An alternative wholesome and clean—

Bible dress-up for this Halloween.

Expecting bathrobes and wigs,

We got demons in pigs,

And chaos that was unforeseen.

offering

A dilemma for Pastor Kate:

Lotto tickets in the offering plate.

She preached gambling's a sin...

But...if these were a win...

Well, how nice for the State to donate.

blueprints

New buildings and plans were discussed

As the church built up a big trust.

But now they're in debt,

Expectations unmet,

And the pews are all covered in dust.

time

'Twas the hour for church bells to chime,

Ol' Ned was there before nine.

But Dee was irate

As they showed up late,

Despising Daylight Savings Time.

holy

The preacher, he caused a big scene

In the Church of the Nazarene.

He would preach to "live holy,"

But played soccer as goalie,

And skipped church to be with the team.

doorbells

The church had a greeter named Norman;

All handshakes and smiles, quite the doorman!

But at home he would hide

From the stranger outside,

Not answering the door to a Mormon.

communion

It's time for the holy cuisine.

The table prepared crisp and clean.

You're getting the gist,

But it's not Eucharist.

I'm talking donuts served with caffeine.

family

The Johnsons just could not deny it,

Attending church was causing a riot.

All giggles and noise

And smuggled-in toys.

And worship was "shush" and "be quiet"!

committed

Mark and Kira liked to volunteer.

They served their church with good cheer.

On their third anniversary

Mark signed up for the nursery.

And Kira, 'twas said, shed a tear.

silenced

Pastor Jon worked hard on his sermon.

His delight was to see people squirmin.'

But his study had mice,

And his notes paid the price.

It was condemning words for those vermin.

meetings

The church had to form a committee,

To plan an outreach in the city.

But Rob showed up late,

And Jan would not wait,

So nothing got done, it's a pity.

authority

God's law to Moses was known

Through text found on tablets of stone.

Now commandments are blurred;

Some folks say they're absurd,

According to texts on my phone.

mentors

For counsel they would meet in pairs,

Share coffee and leave time for prayers.

But when Billy Flynn

Confessed all his sin,

Elder Tom began having nightmares.

fundraiser

The church ladies held a bazaar

To raise funds for missions afar.

There's baking and crafts,

A creche with giraffes…

Which everyone found quite bizarre!

announcements

The publication proclaimed the great need—

Volunteer please, and someone to lead,

Bible study midweek,

Finances look bleak.

The church bulletin—that no one will read.

redundant

The praise chorus had a great beat,

But the lyrics—they seemed incomplete.

We sang "God is great,"

A good thing to state,

But we'd sing it ten times—then repeat!

slain

Jubilant Jill loved to praise,

Her arms swiftly would raise.

But Jack stood too close,

Now with bloodied nose,

Her worship left him in a daze.

brewing

Some church members threatened to quit.

The coffee, they claimed, was unfit.

"This store brand must end—

We demand gourmet blend."

'Twas the reason behind the church split.

rejoicing

Shy Sue had a restrictive diet.

Communion...reluctant to try it.

But then Reverend Ted

Offered gluten free bread.

She partook—then could not stay quiet!

servant

Pastor Kyle was lamenting his job
As his head was starting to throb.
He was squeezing a sponge,
Had a toilet to plunge.
"I was hired to preach, not to swab!"

benediction

All the churches in town are in play

To get to the Hometown Buffet.

With our service at nine,

We can be first in line.

So hurry up Pastor, and pray!

the end

acknowledgments

She corrects all my typos and spelling

Gives input that is quite compelling

Her name is Lorie,

The best part of my story.

I'm grateful, and that is worth telling.

About Chuck Neighbors

Chuck Neighbors is an actor and writer. For over 45 years he has toured throughout North America as well as 18 countries around the world. His most popular show, a one-man dramatic adaptation of Charles Sheldon's classic **In His Steps**, has been featured on radio and television and performed before thousands of audiences. Chuck has performed in theaters, churches, gymnasiums, airplane hangars and even on board a submarine. As a writer, Chuck's published works include 11 books of theater scripts including his best-selling **What Would Jesus Do? Playbook** (Lillenas) and the 6-volume series **Power Plays** (Baker Books). He authored **Drama Now** (Lillenas), a drama workshop he has taught in hundreds of churches, schools and conferences. Chuck is married to Lorie and they make their home in Salem, Oregon.

Made in the USA
Middletown, DE
17 November 2019